Oyinkan Braithwaite gained a degree in Creative Writing and Law at Kingston University. Her first book, *My Sister, the Serial Killer*, was a number-one bestseller. It was

Also by Oyinkan Braithwaite

My Sister, the Serial Killer

THE BABY IS MINE

OYINKAN BRAITHWAITE

atlantic·fiction

First published in paperback in Great Britain in 2021 by
Atlantic Books, an imprint of Atlantic Books Ltd.

10 9 8 7 6 5 4 3 2 1

A CIP catalogue record for this book is available from the
British Library.

Paperback ISBN: 978 1 83895 256 3
E-book ISBN: 978 1 83895 257 0

Printed and bound by CPI Group (UK) Ltd, Croydon CR0 4YY
Typeset by www.benstudios.co.uk

Atlantic Books
An imprint of Atlantic Books Ltd
Ormond House
26–27 Boswell Street
London
WC1N 3JZ

www.atlantic-books.co.uk

For my grandmother –
Mrs Florence Olubosola Oduntan
You were the first person to pay me
for my writing, thank you

Chapter One

I was living with Mide (she of the wide hips and kinky hair) when we heard the news. The Nigerian government wanted us to join the world and go into lockdown. So we did. We stayed home.

I didn't mind. Mide had a beautiful flat in Ikoyi looking over the Lagoon. She had large French windows, so light was always streaming in and bouncing off her many mirrors. We fell into a routine. She liked to cook for me, I liked letting her. We would eat and then we would part for a few hours to check our emails and join Zoom meetings, before coming together again in the evenings. We were happy.

So I wasn't expecting to be woken up at one in the morning, by a phone glowing just two inches from my face. Had she been holding it there till I woke up, or had she called my name?

'What is this?' she asked. Her words were half cry, half bark, so I knew something was wrong.

I squinted at the bright light. The phone in her hand was mine, and it was open on a WhatsApp chat from a week ago. How had I forgotten to delete it?

'You went through my phone?' I asked. I didn't know what else to say. I was still rubbing the sleep from my eyes, still trying to work out how she knew my password.

'I did. And I'm glad I did, because you are a liar and a cheat!'

She dropped the phone beside me and leapt from our bed. I scooped up my phone, deleted the messages and photos, and scrambled after her.

'I can explain,' I told her. I couldn't. I said all the things you were supposed to say – *It meant nothing. It was a mistake. It had happened before things got serious between us.* But my words were only making her angrier.

'They warned me about you, but I didn't listen,' she said as she flung open the wardrobe and began dragging out my shirts and trousers.

'Haters. All of them. Babe, we can work through this. Every relationship has its ups and downs.'

She laughed. 'You are incredible, Bambi, really. One of a kind. But I'm not the one you are going to make a fool of. I want you out of my house!'

This was starting to look serious. I tried a different approach. 'Babe, calm down. I can't even go anywhere right now. We are on lockdown, remember?'

I only just managed to dodge one of my shoes. I decided that maybe a little space *was* best. I gathered my clothes and stuffed them into a bag, promising her I would call. She reacted by unlocking the front door and holding it open. I got into my car and backed out of her driveway for the first time in two weeks.

The question now was, where would I go? Mide didn't leave me with enough time to work that out, so I was just driving up and down empty streets. I tried to call Uche, who I had shared a flat with before I moved in with Mide. But he didn't pick up, and in any case, he had already told me someone had taken my room. My sister would have been the easiest option, but she and her family hadn't made it back from their holiday before Nigeria closed its borders. So they were forced to extend their stay in an Airbnb, spending money they hadn't planned on spending. I might have called her anyway, for a little bit of comfort, but she would only snort at the mess I had landed myself in.

'It serves you right,' she would say. 'Maybe this will teach you to keep it in your pants.'

Even though I had told her, time and time again, that a man was not meant to be tied to only one woman. It went against the laws of nature itself. And who was I to argue with nature?

Chapter Two

My grandfather's house was one of the few left on Awolowo Road. He had bought it just before the civil war and left the property to Uncle Folu in his will.

I hadn't been to the house in a while, but it was only a ten-minute drive from Mide's flat and I knew where they kept a spare key. I imagined it would be empty – Uncle Folu was the first person I knew to die from the virus, and I didn't think my aunt would stay in the house on her own. And since she had a newborn baby, it was far more likely that she would have gone to stay with a relative. I would hang out at the old bungalow till the lockdown was over.

There was no gateman to open the gate for me, so I lifted the bolts myself and pushed the old creaking gates, until the gap was wide enough. I drove the car in and turned the engine off. Nothing stirred, except the large palm trees that hid the bungalow from view. I walked round to the back of the house, skipping over the mangoes that had ripened long ago and fallen to the ground. They were starting to rot. I lifted the mat in front of the kitchen door, and picked up the silver key. I went into the kitchen.

The house was in darkness. I flicked the light switch but nothing happened – there was no electricity. I used the torch from my phone to search the drawers till I found a candle and a box of matches. Without electricity, I wouldn't be able to charge my phone, so I didn't want to waste the battery.

I warmed the bottom of the candle with the flame from the match, so it melted a little and would stick to a saucer. That way I could carry it without having the wax drip onto my skin.

A door shut and I almost dropped the candle. But unless the old bungalow had ghosts now, it was safe to say my aunt was home. I should have called ahead. I lit the candle and went out of the kitchen and down the hallway to the dining room. I was heading to the heart of the house.

Suddenly the door to the guest bathroom opened and startled me, forcing me to take a couple of steps back. Aunty Bidemi popped out. She squeaked in terror when she saw me. I lifted the candle a little, so she could get a proper look at my face.

'It's me, Aunty.'

'Bambi?'

'The one and only.'

I could make her out as the light flickered – her short frame, large hips and the long wig glued to her head – so unlike Mide's natural sexy afro.

'Why are you here? Haven't you heard about the lockdown?' Aunty Bidemi asked, squinting at me.

'The lease for my place had come to an end, and the landlord was being unreasonable. You know how people are these days ...'

She didn't respond for a moment, a moment in which I worried that I would soon be back in my car. As I looked at her, I noticed her wig was skewed slightly to the left, and it probably hadn't been combed in weeks. It was straw-like and tangled in places. Her grief was heavy on her still. I tried to remember if I had called her to tell her that I was sorry for her loss.

'Well, maybe it is a good thing you are here,' she sighed. She opened the living-room door, I followed her in.

The room was softly lit by a battery-powered lantern. The walls were covered with pictures of children and grandchildren that my grandfather had collected. Above the TV was the picture of me after my graduation, hanging over the one of my sister. The old-world sofas were covered with large cloths, so they wouldn't gather dust, and so was the piano. And there was a woman in the room. Even though she had her back to us, I could tell who she was by the shape of her hips and her long strong legs. Esohe turned and our eyes met. I was confused. I had never expected to see the two women in the same room.

'Bambi, this is Esohe,' said Aunty Bidemi.

Should I admit that I knew her?

I cleared my throat. 'Hello.'

'Hi.'

We stood there, with our little sources of light revealing our dull faces. I was tempted to blow my candle out, in case my face gave away my thoughts. Seeing Esohe, here, when my aunt was also in the house, was strange. There were so many questions I wanted to ask, but I could ask none of them without revealing too much. And I did not want to be thrown out of two houses in one day.

'Are you hungry?' asked Aunty Bidemi. 'Esohe, get Bambi some food.'

Esohe put her hands on her bony hips and pressed her lips together. She was wearing a T-shirt and leggings, which was a sharp contrast to Aunty Bidemi's shapeless bubu. 'I'm tired.'

Aunty Bidemi massaged the lines in her forehead and stretched her lips into a smile. It was a gesture I knew from my angry teen years. I could guess her next words.

'I'm not asking for too much, am I?'

Esohe shrugged. 'I'll go and prepare it. But you cannot treat me like I'm the house girl.'

She passed by me. She smelt of mango and mint. I felt my muscles tense. I decided against following her. I turned back to find Aunty Bidemi staring at me, as if trying to read my mind. She smiled.

'Come, come and see the baby, Bambi.'

It was then that I noticed the cot.

Chapter Three

Aunty Bidemi was smiling at me, waiting for me to look into the cot and make goo-goo sounds. I went up to the cot and peered in.

The baby looked like a baked potato.

I wanted to be able to say it was cute, but I couldn't work out if it was a boy or a girl. They had dressed it in white, which did not help. It was awake and it reached for me with its tiny fingers.

'Congratulations, Aunty. E ku ewu omo.' I told her in Yoruba, congratulating her on surviving the risks that came with childbirth. I had meant to call her and Uncle Folu when I got news of the baby; but I hadn't gotten round to it. Still, I knew how long she had tried for a child, and I was happy for her.

She turned to me, blinked and then smiled. Aunty Bidemi had a sweet smile – her lips would push her cheeks up, her cheeks would flatten her eyes, so that they became near slits. It was good to see that, even after all she had been through, she could still smile.

'E se o,' she replied. 'Do you want to carry him?'

A boy then. She didn't give me a chance to refuse. She scooped him up, and passed him over to me. I had just enough time to put down the candle and twist my arms into an awkward hammock. He stared at me. It appeared he knew I was a stranger. His white T-shirt had written across it – *My father is a hero* – which I found incredibly sad.

'His name is Remi,' she told me, even though I hadn't asked. 'He likes you.'

'Hmmm.'

'Does he look like Folu?'

I looked for my uncle in his face, but I couldn't see anything about him that was familiar to me. His hair was pitch black and curly, slicked onto his head. He tugged at the thin silver chain that dangled from my neck. He clearly had no clue how expensive that chain was. I gently lifted it free from his fingers and handed him over to his mum.

'He is very cute,' I told her and she gave me a wobbly smile. Was she going to cry? I grabbed my candle from the side table and excused myself quickly.

I walked down one of the long corridors, the sound of my footsteps echoing off the tiles, to the room that was the furthest from the living room and kitchen. I passed three bedrooms and a secondary hallway to reach it. I liked the privacy there.

I sat on the bed, and wondered for the hundredth time which of my grandfather's four wives had decorated the rooms. It seemed to me that she had picked the ugliest wallpaper that she could find. Here, in my room, it was a weird mix of mustard and green. Esohe's leggings had been green. Why on earth was she at the house?

My T-shirt stuck to my skin and I was reminded of how hot it was. So I peeled it off and tossed it on to the chair. I checked my phone to see if Mide had come to her senses. She hadn't. I blew out the candle and closed my eyes.

Chapter Four

I woke up feeling hungry and sticky, and realized that the house was humming with activity. I could hear the low drone of kitchen appliances and the static from the TV. Electricity had returned, for now at least. I climbed out of bed, stretched my tight muscles and turned on the air con. I stood just below it and the blast of cool air soothed my body and soul.

There was a soft knock on the door.

'Come in.'

'Help me open the door, please.'

I opened the door and found Aunty Bidemi holding a tray of food. I took it from her and set it on my bed.

'Thank you. You should have told me it was ready, I would have come to collect it myself.'

'Ah no. You are a guest. We must treat you accordingly.' Her gaze slipped away from my face and down to my bare chest. I grabbed my T-shirt and pulled it on.

There were beads of sweat on her forehead,

nose and upper lip, where I could also make out a faint moustache. She really wasn't looking after herself. I still remembered what she had looked like as a young bride. I was only ten then and to me she was a Disney princess. Or three Disney princesses – even back then, her waist had not been small. She sat down on my chair and it creaked in protest. She wiped her forehead, and her wig shifted a little further to the left.

Outside, I could hear the crowing of a cock. I glanced at my phone. It was early still. I wanted to eat alone, but she did not seem to be in a hurry to leave. The meal was beans and plantain. I sat on my bed, took up the tray and began to eat. I would have waited for her to go, but I was hungry. Perhaps when she had caught her breath, she would—

'Esohe was your uncle's ... mistress.'

I lowered the fork back to the plate. I tried to look shocked.

'Really?!'

Chapter Five

The first time I met Esohe was at a bar. It was a place I went to when I didn't want to bump into anyone I knew. It was out of the way, drab and always heavy with the fog of cigarette smoke and weed. That night I walked in and nodded across the room to Dotun, the barmaid. She gave me two thumbs-up and set about getting my regular order.

I headed to the corner seat that I usually took – it gave you the perfect view of the bar and the entrance – but it was occupied.

'Uncle Folu?'

He looked up at me and frowned. He wasn't pleased to see me. The girl sitting opposite him and with her back to me twisted around. I was struck by how long and thin she was, like a praying mantis. She didn't seem like the type of girl you would cheat on your wife with – her breasts were tiny. We both had a liking for curvy, full-figured women and she was not that. Maybe she wasn't having an affair with my

15

uncle. Perhaps I had stumbled across a business meeting. But who held business meetings in a place like this?

I returned my uncle's grim look with a smile and slipped into the seat beside him. I held out my hand to the woman.

'My name is Bambi. Who do I have the pleasure of meeting?' She shook my hand. The pandemic hadn't yet arrived to make us afraid of physical contact. She smiled at me, but she looked at him for approval. Definitely an affair, then. He gave her a stiff nod. And we turned back to one another.

'I'm Esohe.'

I studied her, trying to understand what had attracted him to her. She seemed younger than me, which made her at least twenty years younger than Uncle Folu. Perhaps that was what drew him. Dotun brought my food to the table.

'Add it to my uncle's tab, please,' I told her. 'Esohe, have you ordered?'

'No, I—'

'Ah! Dotun, please bring her your best goat meat, and ... would you like Chapman? They make great Chapman here ... excellent! And Chapman, Dotun!'

I knew Uncle Folu would have a go at me later, but I was enjoying myself. And Esohe was smiling a little. She could tell I was messing with him. Maybe she was glad that he was being made to squirm.

But despite how annoyed my uncle was, he knew that what had taken place would not leave the four walls of the dingy bar. There were rooms upstairs that he no doubt intended to make use of, but that was not my business. My uncle was a good husband – he gave his wife whatever she asked for and he had not hassled her over her failure to give him a child. If he needed to relieve the stress every now and again, who was I to judge?

Chapter Six

'Bambi, I thought he had put all that nonsense behind him. Why are men like this?' asked Aunty Bidemi.

Did she expect me to speak for all men, or just for Uncle Folu? This was not the time to deliver my speech about how it was unnatural to expect a man to love just one woman. Instead, I tried to think of something comforting to say. She was leaning forward on the edge of my chair. The air conditioner had begun to cool her. She was sweating less.

'Well …'

'Am I not attractive again?'

She was no spring chicken. But she still had some charming features – her smile for one, and her skin was pillow soft. She may have had one fat fold too many, but the baby weight was probably to blame for that.

'If I was your age, I would be lucky to have you,' I told her.

She sighed and the heaviness of her breath

caused her breasts to jiggle. She had always had a mother's bosom.

'So long as a man has money, a man does not age. Not like a woman.'

I reached out and patted her on the shoulder. 'Uncle Folu loved you. Whatever he did with Esohe, it was not serious.' But she shook off my hand.

'What kind of love is that? Do you know she cannot even make his favourite soup? Folu used to complain and complain until I learnt how to make egusi soup the way he liked it. And this girl just …'

Her voice cracked.

'Why is she here, Aunty Bidemi?'

Aunty Bidemi breathed another heavy jiggly sigh. 'She was pregnant and had nowhere to go.'

'Esohe was pregnant?!' My voice came out a little high pitched. I coughed to clear my throat. I must have misheard.

'Yes, she was. But she lost the baby, poor girl. And before I could ask her to please leave, the lockdown started.'

'Hmmm.' I tried to take in this news. How many months was it since the last time I saw Esohe? Surely, she would have told me if—

'Are you OK?'

'Huh? Oh, yeah. It's just the heat.' I fanned myself with my hand to back up my story.

Aunty Bidemi stood up.

'I'll let you eat in peace.'

I'm not certain I replied to her.

Chapter Seven

I needed a shower. I went to my car to collect my things and then headed to the bathroom, wrapped in my towel, and carrying my wash bag. It looked like it had been a while since the bathroom had been cleaned. I could see marks in the sink and on the floor.

There was a black bucket sitting in the bathtub waiting to be filled with water, so I could have an old-school shower. I turned on the tap and waited for the bucket to fill. I had poured the first bowl of water on my body, when I heard a scream.

I grabbed my towel and dashed out of the bathroom. The women were shouting and I followed the sound to Aunty Bidemi's room. I twisted the handle. The door didn't give way immediately. Sometimes you had to wrestle with doors in the old house. I used my shoulder.

They were like two snakes entangled on the floor, tearing at each other's clothing on the wine-red sheepskin carpet. A blue ceramic bowl was in pieces, with peeled oranges scattered along with it. The baby was on the edge of the bed crying, his nappy half open. I controlled my anger and went straight to the baby, stepping over the fighting women and lifting him into my arms. I freed up a hand and grabbed Esohe's arm, dragging her off my aunt. The towel slipped and I let her go just in time to prevent it from exposing me completely.

'What the hell is going on here?' I shouted.

They looked up at me, as though surprised to see me there. Aunty Bidemi's wig had been knocked off and could have been mistaken for a bush rat on the floor. I repeated my question, slowly.

Esohe stood. She was a couple of inches taller than me, so I was forced to lift my head up to meet her eyes. There was a nasty gash on her arm, but she didn't appear to notice that she was bleeding. She pointed at the angry, wailing baby in my arms.

'That is my baby!'

'You are crazy,' spat Aunty Bidemi. She crawled to the bed and hoisted herself up. 'And I want you out! I want you out now!'

Esohe made a grab for a shard of the broken bowl and pointed it at Aunty Bidemi, forcing the older woman to stumble back. I put myself between them.

'If you attack my aunt, you will have me to deal with.' Esohe didn't try to call my bluff. She lowered her weapon. She was breathing heavily. Her blonde braids were sticking to her dark skin.

'He is *my* baby,' she repeated.

She opened her arms, as though she expected me to just hand the baby over to her. I held him a little more tightly. It was like holding a pillow.

'I'm sorry that you lost your baby, Esohe, I'm sure it was very—'

'Are you mad? I did not lose my baby. Is that what *she* told you?' Her voice was getting louder and louder. Aunty Bidemi stepped out from behind me.

'The girl is unstable. Give me the baby.' I nearly handed him over, but she looked more unwell than the woman she was accusing. Her wig was lying trampled on the ground and I could see the messy cornrows on her head, dotted with dandruff. Her mascara had run down her face, so she looked like she was crying black goo. And I could not escape the fact that *both* women had chosen their petty fight over the safety of the baby.

Besides, he had gone quiet. There was no real reason to hand him over. As if he agreed, he grabbed hold of my finger.

'She is the one with a dead baby!' Esohe hissed.

'Are you calling my aunty a liar?'

'So, I'm the one that is a liar?'

'Don't talk to her, Bambi. Just hand the baby over.' Aunty Bidemi reached for him.

'No! No!' Esohe screamed. 'He is my baby!'

The baby began to cry again. I resisted the urge to throw Esohe out of the room and lock the door.

'Calm down! Look, this isn't 1000 BC. You can't just claim a baby. There are DNA tests now.'

'Fine. Let's do a DNR test.'

'DNA.'

'Whatever. Let's do it.'

This was an interesting turn of events. I turned to Aunty Bidemi. She shrugged and folded her arms.

'That's fine with me. Let's do it.'

Esohe had a pretty fine poker face for someone who was clearly bluffing. I didn't really want to waste anybody's time by asking for a DNA test, but perhaps that was the only way to solve the problem.

'OK ... I'll call a few hospitals and get back to you.'

'No oh. You must make the calls in front of me so I know there is no funny business.'

'Fine. Let's meet in the living room in ten minutes. I need to put on some clothes and get my phone.' I walked out of the room, taking the baby with me before either of them had a chance to protest. By the time we got to my room, he had fallen asleep.

Chapter Eight

The baby and I were both pretty much butt naked, so I placed him on the bed and covered him up to his neck with a blazer, before dressing myself with boxers, a vest and sweat pants. I sat on the bed next to him. He was so small. His skin was a deep brown, except for a yellow birthmark on his stomach. I touched the soft curls growing on his head.

Happy that I had enough clothes on, I unplugged my phone from the charger, picked him up again and headed to the living room. Luckily, Aunty Bidemi was there with a nappy and a babygrow. I gave him to her and she wiped his bottom, powdered his bum, and snapped on his nappy as though she were some kind of ninja.

Esohe walked in and narrowed her eyes. I could see she was tempted to walk over and pick him up but she sat on the chair nearest the door.

'Make the call,' she said.

I called my friend Uche. He was a doctor and I knew he would be willing to help me out. I put the call on loudspeaker.

'Guy, how far?'

'I dey,' I told him. 'How are you? How are you coping?'

'Man, we are taking it one day at a time. Sorry I missed your call the other day. I hope you are not sick.'

'No, no. I'm fine. I just need your advice. Do you have a minute?'

'Yes. Hit me.'

'How can one go about getting a DNA test?'

He sighed. 'I knew this day would come.'

Esohe smirked and I took the phone off loudspeaker.

'It isn't a paternity test that I want,' I hissed.

'Oh?'

'Put it back on loudspeaker,' said Esohe. I slowly thumbed the speaker button.

'I'm trying to find out how someone can get a maternity test.'

'Now, *that's* interesting. But to be honest, this is not the time. The labs here are swamped testing for the virus. A maternity test would be very low priority. I would suggest waiting till the pandemic blows over and checking then.'

'Where would we go to do the test, once this is over?'

He named a couple of places and I wrote them down in my phone's note app. As I said goodbye, he told me that he would need the full story when things had gone back to normal. I smiled. His thirst for gossip was the same as ever.

'Maybe we should try calling a hospital?' said Aunty Bidemi.

We tried three hospitals, and they all said that it was not the time to be asking for a maternity test. Esohe was pacing up and down.

'What's going to happen now?' she asked.

'Look, the hospitals and medical labs are overwhelmed. So I think the best thing we can do now is try to live together in some kind of harmony, until we have a chance to do the test. After all, none of us is going anywhere any time soon.'

She stopped pacing long enough to groan and stamp her foot, and then she was gone.

Chapter Nine

I spent the rest of the day in my bedroom. I fired up my laptop, watched *The Platform* on Netflix, and then did some freelance accounting for a company that would clearly have to file for bankruptcy soon. They wouldn't be the first or the last. The lockdown had ruined many businesses.

I did not leave until the evening, when the electricity was cut off again. I closed the lid of my laptop, lit the candle, and went to the living room. Aunty Bidemi was feeding the baby. He looked peaceful. Esohe was not in the room.

'You must be hungry,' said Aunty Bidemi, looking up at me and smiling. 'Dinner is almost ready.'

'Thank you. But I actually wanted to ask about the generator.'

She shook her head. 'It overheated. And nobody is moving around right now, so we can't get it fixed.'

My shoulders dropped. I had left a place of

light and air and regular love-making, to come to ... a house of low ceilings, dust, mould and endless rugs. And now there was no generator. The heat would become as thick as a blanket and, at night, the mosquitoes would descend.

'He's asleep,' she said softly, breaking into my thoughts. I watched as she lowered the baby gently into his cot. 'Go to the dining room, Bambi, I'll check on the stew.'

'Do you have no one here to help you?'

'No. It is just us.'

'But what about the help?'

'Don't mind them, most of them ran off after ... after your uncle got sick.'

'And the others?'

'What?'

'The ones that didn't run off. What happened to them?'

She sighed. 'The lockdown happened. They wanted to go to their families.' She opened the door and waited for me to walk out, then she left the door slightly open. She went on into the kitchen.

Esohe was already in the dining room. She did not look at me, but I could sense her anger in the stiffness of her expression. Her lips were pressed together and there were lines on her forehead.

'Hey.'

She sat up, crossed her arms and seemed to wait for me to say something more. She was wearing a large T-shirt that fell to her knees. I couldn't help but wonder if she was wearing shorts underneath. Her braids fell on her shoulders and onto the table. I thought about what I could say.

Aunty Bidemi bustled in with a dish of food, and I got up to help her. Esohe was busy pouring herself a glass of wine. She didn't fill anyone else's glasses. When we were all seated, we started serving up in silence. The only sounds were the squeak of cutlery against china. They didn't say anything to one another, so I was forced to pass the dishes between them.

I took a forkful of the rice, and then another. But when I began to chew, I felt something gritty between my teeth, something unpleasant. I spat the rice out into my palm. There was sand in the food. Seconds later, Aunty Bidemi did the same.

'What is wrong?' asked Esohe. She leant over to peer at her own plate, pushing the food about with her fork. 'Wait ... what is this?'

'You tell us, Esohe,' said Aunty Bidemi in a low, grim voice.

'What? How ...? I didn't do this!'

'So it was some spirit that did it?!' asked Aunty Bidemi.

Esohe looked at me. 'Bambi … *you* don't think that I–'

I cut her off. 'How come you didn't eat it?'

'I was going to eat it! I do not rush food into my mouth like you people.'

Aunty Bidemi stood up, toppling her chair over. 'I have had enough!' she roared. 'Esohe, I want you to leave. Please, pack your things and go.'

Esohe's eyes widened. She seemed surprised that she was being thrown out, which was odd, considering the battle these two were in. I watched as Esohe's mouth opened and shut. But then her eyes narrowed and she tilted her head to one side. We waited for her to say something. And finally she did.

'No.'

'What?'

'I'm not going anywhere. In fact, the house belongs to my baby and me now. This is Folu's gift to us.'

I only just managed to hold Aunty Bidemi back as she leapt for Esohe. And maybe if I hadn't been holding her back, I would have leapt for her myself. Who did she think she was?! But Esohe didn't even flinch. She got up slowly, tossed back her braids and left the room. I could feel Aunty Bidemi's body trembling. She was crying.

'What did I do to deserve this?'

Nothing. We were all just creatures of our base natures.

Chapter Ten

In the end, I had to make do with a few slices of bread.

It felt as though I had been at the house for six months, but it was still only my first day at the old bungalow. And despite the fact that it was almost midnight, the cock was crowing again. I peered out of my window, which let me see about a quarter of the garden, but I couldn't see the noisy beast. I would have to ask my aunt about him in the morning.

I lay back on my bed and stared into the darkness. I thought of Mide and how comfortable she would be in her king-sized bed. But perhaps she would be a little lonely, too. She hadn't reached out to me yet, but she would sooner or later.

Just as I was idly beginning to wonder what Mide might be wearing in bed – whether it was hot enough for her to sleep naked, perhaps – Esohe's face came to mind, ruining my train of thought. I remembered the frantic look in her eyes when she insisted the baby was hers. But I had seen Aunty Bidemi with her swelling belly and her glow. Esohe was bound to cause more trouble if she went on living with us. I would have to handle her in the morning.

There was no sound in the house – except for the near constant crowing of the cock, the shuffle of the bedsheet, and my body would jolt itself awake, whenever I heard the soft whine of the mosquito. And now the crying. I could hear Remi bawling and the sound was like a thousand needles being shoved into my ear.

I jumped up from the bed. I had had very little to do with babies, but you could tell when an animal was in distress. Only, when I turned the handle of my room, it wouldn't give. This wasn't the time for the house to play up with its rusty hinges and swollen wood. I shook the door. I didn't have the patience I usually had. I shouted for Aunty Bidemi, and then for Esohe but no one came.

I tried the door again, harder this time. Was it possible that I was locked in? And why would no one just pick the child up? I could hear them now, the two women, their raised voices, but the baby's crying had not stopped. I shouted again, but still nothing. My patience gave out: I rammed my body against the door, and it splintered open.

By the time I got to Aunty Bidemi's room, Remi's cries had only got louder. I opened the door.

The room was dark, except for a candle that was flickering on my aunt's dressing table. There was still no electricity. Aunty Bidemi had the baby in a tight grip in her arms, and Esohe seemed to be trying to loosen that grip. They fought with the baby sandwiched between them. I strode across the room and lifted the baby from my aunt's arms.

There was something wet and dark on his face. It was blood, almost black in the candlelight. I felt a little woozy but I managed not to loosen my grip on him.

'Bambi, she—' began Esohe.

'Don't,' I said. I ran a thumb gently over his cheek, wiping away the blood. More sprang from wounds in the skin. 'Did neither of you think about cleaning his wounds?'

They both stayed silent.

I held him close to me and headed for the bathroom. The women followed me quietly. I pulled the first-aid box down from the cupboard and began cleaning the cuts of the tearful baby. I could see the marks more clearly now. Someone had made three sharp cuts on either side of his face, but they weren't meant to hurt him. They were tribal marks.

Still, I felt my rage bubbling to the surface. We didn't do this in our family. I didn't think anyone did it any more. And it would cause people to judge the child before they even got a chance to know him. He deserved better than this. I wiped his tears with my finger. He was a little warm and plenty helpless.

'Which of you did this?'

'It was her,' said Esohe. 'She was the one.'

Aunty Bidemi folded her arms. 'He is my son. In my family, we—' At least she had saved me time by admitting it. But her voice grated on my nerves.

'I couldn't care less what they do in your family. You married into *this* family. You follow *our* rules.'

I expected Aunty Bidemi to protest. But it was Esohe who spoke next.

'See? She is mad. See how she ruined my baby's face.'

'It isn't ruined,' I told her. I was tired of both of them and I wanted so badly to sleep.

'She had no right to do this. She had no right!'

The baby was still crying. I did what I could do to soothe him. I rocked him gently.

'Get me milk,' I ordered.

Aunty Bidemi left the room.

'Bambi—' Esohe began.

I held up a warning hand. 'Stop. I'm not interested. If you stay here you shut up.' She sat down on the toilet seat and didn't say another word. When Aunty Bidemi returned fifteen minutes later with his bottle, Remi was much calmer. He seemed to like it when I rocked him steadily back and forth, his small hand gripping my finger. He took the milk greedily.

'I wasn't trying to hurt him,' mumbled Aunty Bidemi. Her hands were behind her back and I could tell she was twisting her fingers. I was almost tempted to comfort her, but when I opened my mouth, the words that came out were –

'But you did.'

I walked out of the bathroom with him still in my arms, just as the power came back on and light flooded the house. At least as much of it as the dim bungalow would allow – some of the bulbs needed to be changed. But, at least, we could see our way back to my room and I would be able to turn my air conditioner on.

'Let me put him in his cot,' Aunty Bidemi called after me. 'I have moved it back to my room.'

I looked down at the baby, now asleep in my arms.

'He will sleep with me tonight.'

Chapter Eleven

I lay wide awake in the dark. I could hear Remi's light breathing beside me. What if I rolled over and stopped him breathing? What if *he* rolled over and fell? I hadn't seen him roll, but just because I hadn't seen it, didn't mean it couldn't happen. It amazed me that he was able to sleep at all. The cock was crowing loud and clear into the night. But when I looked out of my window, I could not see it.

Eventually, I gave up on the idea of sleep. I sat up slowly, so I didn't disturb him and called my sister. She picked up just as I was about to give up.

'Will you shut up?! Mummy is on the phone. Hey, Bambi, what's up? How are you?'

'I'm fine.'

'You sure? You sound weird. What time is it there?'

'Late.'

She sighed. 'I don't know why you call and then give me one-word answers. How is Uche?'

'He is ok. But I'm actually staying at the old bungalow.'

'Oh! How is Aunty Bidemi? Is she doing OK? I can't imagine what it must be like to lose your husband!'

'I think she is ... coping.'

'Gosh! She is strong. And how is the baby? He is so handsome, isn't he?'

'Wait. You've seen a picture?'

'Yes. Oh gosh, these children are driving me up the wall. Why did I have four of them? What was I thinking?'

'Bukky, focus. You said you saw a picture of the baby.'

'Yes. Aunty Bidemi sent a broadcast when she gave birth. It is really sad she couldn't have the naming ceremony. But these are the times we are in, I guess. Soji, come say hi to your uncle. *Hi, uncle Bambi*!' I rolled my eyes. She was using her baby voice now and talking for her child. It was this kind of thing that stopped me from calling more often.

'Look, can you help me find that picture?'

'Why? Say, hi, Uncle Bambi. *Hi, Uncle Bambi*.'

'Just please, send it.' I ended the call as quickly as I could and cut the line. Peace once again took over.

I looked at Remi. He *was* cute. One day he would probably break a thousand hearts. I put one pillow on either side of him on the bed and then, smoothing my blazer out on the floor, I lay down on it and shut my eyes. The crowing started up again.

Chapter Twelve

The next morning, when I returned Remi to his mother, I was calmer. I knew she had meant him no real harm. And she clearly hadn't given someone tribal marks before – the cuts were too shallow to leave a lasting mark on his face. In a few months, there would be no trace of them. I kept that info to myself.

Aunty Bidemi was in the living room, and I could see that she had been crying – she kept sniffing and her face looked puffy. She took Remi from me greedily and I hardened my heart.

'If,' I told her, 'you try something like that again—'

'Bambi, I know you want to help, but I am your aunty and Remi's mother. You cannot talk to me like that.'

'Then behave like someone who has sense.'

'What is the matter with you?' She started crying again. 'Haven't I gone through enough without you disrespecting me on top of everything?!'

'I'm just thinking of the baby.'

'And I'm thinking of him too!'

I lifted up my hands to show I was giving in, and I left her with Remi. I decided to go searching for the cock. I walked through the garden, breathing in the fresh air and the scent of rotting mangoes. I looked through bushes, wondering where a cock might hide out.

I heard a rustling near a line of trees at the back of the house. I slipped in between the trees and found Esohe leaning calmly against a tree trunk, smoking a blunt. She raised an eyebrow and held out the blunt to me. I thought about rejecting it, but only for a moment. She was wearing a black dress that was an inch too short, and traditional beads dangled from around her long neck. I tasted her lips on the joint. We smoked in silence, but I knew the quiet could only last so long.

'I know you know that baby is not her own.'

I took another three or four puffs before I answered her. 'I don't know anything.'

'Her womb is old. She is lucky she even got pregnant.'

'Watch your mouth.'

I took another look at her. Her eyes were red, her lips raw and I felt her body shiver beside mine. All was not well with her. She needed the blunt a hell of a lot more than I did. I gave it back to her.

'Can't you help me out, for old times' sake?'

'I don't know you like that, Esohe.'

Her response was to spit on the ground. 'You are an ass.'

'So I've heard.'

She stormed off, and it was only when she was almost at the door that I remembered I needed to find the cock.

'Hey!' I called after her. 'There is a chicken that keeps crowing. Where is it?'

She didn't bother answering me. She slammed the door behind her.

I was alone once more. Since the cock appeared to be hiding from me, I decided to get in a half-hour of exercise. I felt the heat of the sun on my back as I lowered myself to the ground, slowly, and then lifted myself up again. It had been too long since I had taken the time to work out my muscles and I could feel the strain. Eleven, twelve, thirteen. I cleared my mind and tried to focus instead on the gentle breeze. Twenty, twenty-one, twenty-two. The gravel began to dig into my hands and it quickly became painful, so I switched to star jumps. Otherwise I would have had to go into the house, but the women were in there.

I stood up when I heard the cock crowing again. I walked around to the side passage and down the three stone steps. There it was, twerking its neck and taking itself for a stroll. I could not say why, but it felt good to see it there, walking and squawking; even though it really had no business making noise at 1:05 p.m.

I had had no plan for when I found him. All I knew was that I wanted the crowing to stop. I would make him stop. But now, it was clear to me how pointless my feelings were. He was a beast bound to his nature; he could not stop even if he tried. He would not stop until he was dead.

I went to fetch a slice of bread and broke it into little bits for the cock. It came to me without a dash of fear. It was hard to tell if this was normal, or if perhaps the fact that humans had been off the street for months had made the chicken bolder. After all, they were not known for their long memories.

It paused its mission of informing the world of the time, to have its lunch break, and we hung out together quietly. I stuffed some of the bread into my own mouth. I wondered where the cock had come from and why it had settled here. The garden was mostly barren. The grass was not growing as it had in the past, and no one had taken the time to work out why. My grandfather had not passed on his love of plants to the rest of us.

The cock squawked at me. I was out of bread. It squawked at me again. Our mutual peace seemed to have come to an end. It was flapping its wings at me, and I could tell it was close to attacking me so I stood up. Fair enough, our friendship had formed over food, it made sense that it would be threatened by food too.

I went back to the house.

Chapter Thirteen

I wanted to check on Remi, so I knocked on Aunty Bidemi's door and entered when she answered.

She was sitting on a stool humming, with her breast out. It looked large and heavy, criss-crossed with raised veins. They were big enough to smother a full-grown man, let alone a baby. She made no attempt to cover herself with a cloth.

'Sorry,' I said, spinning around so that I wasn't looking at her. 'I didn't know you were ... I didn't realize he was ... breastfed.'

She laughed behind me. 'Bambi, don't be a child.'

I turned back to her, keeping my eyes well away from her chest area. They had been giving him milk with a bottle the whole time that I had been at the house. I hadn't thought that she might also be breastfeeding him. But at least he was being fed. I, on the other hand, was starving. I mentioned this to Aunty Bidemi.

'You know where the kitchen is, don't you?'

I laughed. 'What happened to "you are a guest"?'

'You can see my hands are full.'

Aunty Bidemi was clearly still angry with me. And I could see from the stormy look on her face that she was going to be stubborn on the matter of my food. I thought about Esohe, but she was probably annoyed at me too.

I spent the first fifteen minutes in the kitchen trying to find where everything was. The old bungalow was not ageing well. Drawers were stuck, paint was peeling from the doors, and it took a couple of tries before I could get the cooker to work.

I took eggs from the fridge and cracked them into a bowl while I gazed out of the kitchen window. The cock was trotting about the driveway and Esohe walked into my view. I wondered whether she was going to smoke another blunt.

I had just found the salt when I happened to glance out of the window again. Esohe was now standing in the middle of the driveway, holding the cock upside down. I dropped the eggs to the ground, and pulled the kitchen door open.

'No, wait!' I shouted, but it was too late. She had already drawn a small knife across its throat, slicing its neck wide open. She dropped the cock and we watched as its body flapped and danced about. Blood spurted from its neck, spraying the ground. It took too many moments for it to realize that it had died. I was no vegetarian, but it made me feel sick. 'What the hell is wrong with you?'

'Have you not noticed we have run out of meat in the house?'

'But still ...'

'But still *what*?' She looked at me and then slowly shook her head. The knife was still tight in her hand. 'It was just a chicken. Grow up.'

Chapter Fourteen

Dinner was rice and chicken.

I pushed the chicken about on my plate. I knew I was being childish, but it was difficult to stop.

'Are you OK?' asked Aunty Bidemi. 'I thought you said you were hungry?'

I looked up. Esohe had already cleared her plate. There had been no sand today, and the women had managed not to abuse each other yet, but my spirits stayed low.

'I'm fine.'

'Are you seriously going to be a baby over this chicken? I can throw it back up for you.' The more you got to know her, the less attractive Esohe became. What had Uncle Folu been thinking?

'That chicken was a gift,' added Aunty Bidemi. 'If we didn't eat it, someone else would have eaten it.'

'Well, I'm glad we are all in agreement,' I replied.

'If you don't want to eat your chicken, give it to me,' said Esohe, twisting her neck at me.

Her neck was long and thin, it reminded me of the cock's neck. Where on earth did all the food she ate go? I pushed my plate away and stood up. 'Fine,' I said. 'Take it. I'm done. I'll go check on the baby.'

'No!' said Esohe. 'It is my turn to look after Efosa!'

'You mean, Remi,' Aunty Bidemi growled.

'That is not his name. His name is Efosa.' I stopped walking. If these women decided to attack and kill each other, I'd be the one left to clean it up. And I had seen enough blood for one day.

Aunty Bidemi snorted, 'That is not a Yoruba name.'

'I am not Yoruba.'

'What does that have to do with anything? Remi is Yoruba.'

'Folu and I agreed—'

Aunty Bidemi clapped her hands furiously as though she were killing a mosquito between them.

'Don't say his name! Don't you dare say his name!'

'I have rights!' Esohe cried.

'Rights? What rights do you have? You were just my husband's slut!'

At this, they both pushed back their chairs and sprang up, facing one another across the table. Esohe's strong, capable hand gripped her fork, while Bidemi held the wine bottle like a club.

I leant my hands on the back of a chair and said calmly, 'Ladies, listen. I will deal with whichever one of you makes the first move. You understand?'

Their bodies were coiled to strike one another, but they remained still. They were glancing at me, waiting to see what I would say next. 'OK, look. This is what we are going to do: you are going to take turns looking after him until this damn lockdown ends. One of you gets him for the morning, the other for the afternoon.' Just then the image of Aunty Bidemi gripping Remi with blood on his face, and then another of Esohe slicing the cock's throat open, played across my mind. 'And at night, I'll look after him.'

The two women lowered their weapons, placed them on the table in front of them. Then they both smirked at the same time. 'You?' said Aunty Bidemi. 'Bambi, what do you know about looking after a baby? Just because you spent one short night with him, doesn't mean—'

'I'll learn.'

Chapter Fifteen

The world outside my bedroom was silent. No crowing. I blew raspberries and Remi gurgled. I had fed him and changed his nappy, but he still would not sleep. I lay next to him, dangling my chain over him while he reached for it. With my free hand, I scrolled through my phone and tried to see what was happening outside the old bungalow. Nothing good. For one, Mide was dissing me on Twitter with sub-tweets –

Never settle.

Just because a man looks good on the outside, doesn't mean he is good on the inside.

Once a cheat, always a cheat.

I liked all her tweets.

I noticed that my sister had also tweeted a few pictures of her kids. It reminded me that she still hadn't sent me the picture that Aunty Bidemi had sent after the baby was born. I dialled her number.

She sounded calmer when she picked up the phone. 'Aunty Bidemi said you are staying with her.'

'I told you that myself when we spoke.'

'Oh. Did you?'

'Yes, I did.' I tried not to be annoyed at her – mothers were all clearly unhinged. 'Could you send me that picture Aunty Bidemi sent you?'

'What picture?'

I held in a breath. 'The one she sent of her baby.'

'Oh, yeah. He is soooo cute.'

'Excellent! Can you—'

'Funso, if you don't get back into bed right now, I swear by my father in heaven that I'll beat you from now till kingdom come ... Sorry, Bambi, you were saying?'

'The picture, can you send it to me?'

'What do you want it for?'

'I want to ... make sure the baby is hers.'

'Excuse you? Who else would the baby belong to?'

I waited a moment, and then let out a breath. 'Uncle Folu's girlfriend is here.'

'Are you serious?'

'Yup.'

'Why don't you guys chase her out?'

'Because the baby might be hers.'

She sighed. 'You are not making sense... Bambi, are you high?'

'No. I'm not high. Just send me the picture.'

'Aunty Bidemi would not say the baby is hers if it wasn't hers. She has been through a lot, Bambi. Don't stir the pot.'

'Are you going to send me the picture or not?'

She sighed. 'I'll have a look for it. But you need to chill with your wild theories, OK?'

I thought about hanging up on her, but since I needed her to do something for me, I gritted my teeth and listened to her news. She told me how their Airbnb was and how long she felt it might be before they could get back home. She had new crazy theories about the virus. She told me how she got her kids to eat their vegetables, and on and on and on. Remi had fallen asleep by the time I was able to get off the phone.

Chapter Sixteen

I opened my eyes. Something was wrong.

Remi was there, his chest was rising and falling. He was safe. But someone had been in the room with us. I was fairly sure that someone had been hovering above us. Their shadow had crept into my sleep. But when I opened my eyes, they were gone.

I switched on the light and looked around the room. My laptop was still on the small desk, along with my phone; my bag lay open on the floor with clothes spilling out and my shoes were lined up neatly against the wall. Maybe one of the women had come in here, since this was where the baby was. Even if I wanted to lock the door, I couldn't – I had broken it the previous evening. Now it barely even shut properly. Still, nothing had been disturbed. I began to relax – perhaps I had dreamt it after all.

Then there was a scream. Again. It sounded like Aunty Bidemi. I briefly thought about taking Remi with me to find out what was going on, but I risked waking him up. I patted the pillows on either side of him and left the room. Aunty Bidemi was standing in the hallway between the dining room and the living room. She had stopped screaming but I could see that she was trembling.

'What's the matter?'

She pointed to the wall. There were uneven streaks of dark red all over the blue-and-white wallpaper, as if smeared on by someone's hands. It looked like blood, it smelt like blood. I felt woozy.

'That girl is a witch,' she hissed. She came towards me, clutching at my vest, but I pushed her off and hung my head between my knees, taking deep, steadying breaths. I didn't do well around blood.

'What are we going to do?' Aunty Bidemi whispered. 'I don't feel safe.'

Just then, the power went off. We were in pitch darkness again, with no candles and no lamps.

'Stay here,' I said to Aunty Bidemi. I staggered along the corridor, still feeling faint, my hand pressed to the walls to guide me in the dark. I needed to get back to Remi.

When I got to the door, I could just make out the figure of Esohe standing by my bed. She had her back to me.

'What do you think you are doing?'

She turned slowly to face me. The baby was in her arms. I could not make out her features or expression.

'I heard all the noise and I came to check on Efosa.'

'Give him to me.'

'Relax, I just—'

'I said, give him to me now.'

She held back, but then she handed him over. She would not have been able to get past me – my whole body filled the doorway.

'What's your problem? I was just making sure that he is OK.'

'You are sick. You are a very sick person. And I don't want you anywhere near him.'

'Is this about the chicken again?'

'Go back to your room.'

'But—'

'Now!'

She fixed me with a glare and then pushed past me, her body briefly coming into contact with my own. I followed her, with the baby in my arms, until she got back to her room. 'It's you people who are sick,' she said to me, before taking one last look at Remi and then closing the door in my face.

Aunty Bidemi was still in the hallway. She had several candles and a bucket of water by her feet. She was using a large sponge to scrub the wall. She deserved better than this.

'I'm sorry,' I said, coming to stand next to her.

'You didn't do this,' she replied, bending over Remi and giving him a light kiss.

'No, but ... I could have done a better job of telling her off when she started her nonsense.'

'I'm scared of her, Bambi.'

'I don't blame you.'

'We have to make sure she doesn't do anything bad to the baby.'

'Look, take him for now; I'll ... I'll clean up the rest of the blood.' She washed her hands in the bucket and dried them on her apron, then lifted the baby from my arms. It took me an hour longer than it probably would have taken her, but I got rid of most of what I guessed was the chicken's blood. Just as I was finishing up, the power came back on, and the bulbs flooded the corridor with a bright orange light.

Chapter Seventeen

It was Esohe's turn to have the baby, but I didn't trust her. I had left him with Aunty Bidemi. For all her flaws, she wasn't the one painting the old bungalow with blood.

So I wasn't too surprised when I heard a knock, which was followed by Esohe slipping lightly into my room.

She didn't look her best. Her braids were loose and brittle, and her face was swollen – from crying, I guessed. But it was hard for me to focus on her face when all she had on was a thin see-through slip.

'What are you wearing?'

'Please,' she said.

She came over to where I was lying on the bed, wearing only boxer shorts. I scrambled away from her to the far side of the bed, but that only seemed to make her more keen to climb in.

'Esohe!' I whispered. 'What are you doing?'

'Please; I'll do anything you want.'

'Aunty Bidemi can come in at any second.'

'This isn't about her. This is about you and me.'

She rubbed her hand along my thigh, slipped a finger into the waistband of my boxers. My body could not help but respond. The best I could manage was a feeble: 'Esohe, stop now.'

'You weren't so coy last year.'

I gripped her wrist, holding it in place, and I waited for her to look up at me. 'I thought you knew that we were never to bring that up.'

'That's why I haven't said anything. You can *trust* me,' she said, before nibbling the tip of my ear.

I began to think about it. We could be done in ten minutes. My aunt was busy with the baby. She would have no reason to come in here. I took Esohe's chin and nudged it towards me, kissing her. Her lips were familiar, soft.

'You see?' she moaned. 'We're good together, you and I. We shouldn't fight so much. We should work together.'

I kissed her again, putting my hands on her thighs, edging up the hem of her slip.

'We could be a family, you know – you, me and the baby.'

The urge left me suddenly. I pushed her back. 'Is that what this is about?'

She shrugged. I was offended. Who did this woman think I was? I had slept with many women during my life, but they had all been willing. More than willing. I hadn't needed to beg or bargain with a single one of them. And this woman thought I would give her a baby, whose safety was uncertain, just because she gave me a moment of pleasure?

'Get out.'

'But Bambi—'

'Are you deaf? Or just stupid? I said, get out!'

'I did not know you were wicked like this,' she spat as she climbed off the bed.

She slammed the door behind her.

I sat on the edge of the mattress and rubbed my temples. I could feel a headache coming on. Beside me, my phone vibrated. It stopped and then started up again. And again. I gave in and looked at the screen – it was Mide. I felt a little hope. It seemed like a lifetime since I had slept through the night, peaceful and calm in her cool bedroom, her naked body next to mine. Perhaps she was calling to offer me paradise.

'Hey—'

'Your wallet,' she said.

'What?'

'You left it here.'

'Oh.'

My hope died. My dismay was total. How dare she tease me by blowing up my phone? It was true that I hadn't seen my wallet in days, but I had no use for it at present, and I had thought it would show up sooner or later.

'What do you want me to do about that now?' I snapped. 'You want me to risk getting the virus by going to yours and then heading back here again?'

The tone of my voice must have surprised her because she was quiet for a moment.

'I'm just letting you know where it is.'

'OK, thanks.' I cut the call.

Chapter Eighteen

I needed a cup of coffee, badly, but the old bungalow didn't offer such treats. A bottle of beer would have to do. On my way to the kitchen I heard rattling and banging coming from Esohe's room. I kept on walking. She was clearly throwing some kind of tantrum and I didn't want to get involved. When I got to the kitchen, I pulled out a bottle from the fridge and opened it against the edge of the counter. I took a deep swig, in the hope that the alcohol would help settle my mood. I looked out of the kitchen window and watched the palms swaying in the breeze. I took another mouthful of beer.

It would have been peaceful, but for the noise coming from Esohe's room, filling the entire house.

'Will you stop it?!' I slammed my hand against her door, on my way back to my room.

'That old witch locked me in!' She twisted the handle from her side. I tried for myself. It was true. She was locked in. 'Help me!'

'Are you sure you didn't lock yourself in by mistake?'

'I don't have any keys to this damn place!'

'OK, OK. Just stop shouting. I will go and talk to her.'

Aunty Bidemi was giving Remi a bath. She propped him up with her hand and stroked his skin gently with a cloth. Remi was developing folds. She would have to get in between them. He looked like a sumo warrior. I sat down on the edge of the bath, cupped a little water into my hand and let it fall on Remi's head. He looked up at me and smiled.

Then I turned to Aunty Bidemi. 'Did you lock Esohe in her room?'

She didn't face me. Instead, she flipped Remi onto his stomach and began to wash his back.

'Yes,' she finally said. 'She is dangerous, Bambi.'

'You can't just keep her locked up, though.'

'Is it after she does something to the baby that we will lock her up?'

I opened my mouth to reply and a yawn escaped instead. Besides, what had I planned on saying? I couldn't dispute Aunty Bidemi's logic. I thought of the presence I had felt in my room the other night, the one that had woken me up. Maybe it had been a dream, but maybe

65

it hadn't. Wasn't it better to be safe than sorry?

'I should have thrown her out a long time ago. I saw her enter your room. That slut!'

I cleared my throat. 'We … I … we didn't.'

'I know. I waited outside your door. She was only there for a few minutes. You are not like your uncle. You are better than him. You won't fall for her tricks.'

She dipped the cloth in the water again and stroked Remi's skin. Her gestures should have been soothing, but her tone was so bitter that I wanted to take him from her arms. She wrapped him in a white towel and planted a kiss on his forehead. My own head was still pounding.

'I need Panadol or Nurofen or something.'

'Check the third drawer next to the fridge.'

I headed back to the kitchen. Esohe was quiet, no doubt because she was waiting for me to rescue her. I found the tablets in the fourth drawer, and also a small bottle of my uncle's whisky on the counter. I took that and the medicine to my room.

Chapter Nineteen

It didn't take Esohe long to realize that help wasn't coming.

I was in the living room with Aunty Bidemi and the baby when Esohe started to shout and scream. Aunty Bidemi did not even flinch. I tried to pretend that the sound was not affecting me either. I flipped a page of a magazine I had picked up off the coffee table. Esohe started pounding on the door again. It sounded as though she was kicking it. My aunt drank her tea.

'Remi looks a lot like you, you know. He has your nose.'

I was beginning to see it. He did have my nose, and I thought the curve of his forehead might be mine. 'It's grandpa's nose,' I told her.

'I hear that they have managed to flatten the curve of the virus,' she said.

'Hmmm.'

'Soon life will be back to normal.'

'Sure. Yes.' I hadn't thought it possible, but Esohe's screams became even louder.

'How is that girl you are dating? The one with the beauty spot? What was her name again?' It didn't matter what her name was. The woman my aunt spoke of was two girlfriends ago.

'I broke up with her.'

'Oh? OK. But you should be thinking about settling down soon. Find a nice girl and marry her.'

'I need to go to the bathroom,' I said.

The sound of Esohe's screams was a little more muffled in my room. I slipped my headphones on, but I knew it was still there – the noise, just beyond the music, waiting for me as soon as I turned the music off. I poured myself a finger of whisky, wincing as I swallowed. My headache had only increased. I needed her to stop making so much noise. I didn't know how Aunty Bidemi could stand it.

I rubbed my eyes. I had lost track of what day and time it was. It felt like I had been at the old bungalow for ever. If the women went on like this, I would grow old beyond my twenty-eight years. Perhaps if I presented Esohe with proof that she wasn't the mother, she would begin to behave normally.

My sister was no use. She still hadn't sent the pictures. I called my brother-in-law. We were not fans of one another – I could hardly be friends with someone who supported Arsenal – but I had to do something.

He picked up on the second ring and said, 'She told you already?'

'Told me what?'

'Oh, never mind. What's up?' His response to my call threw me for a second, but I was not that curious about the goings-on of my sister's life. If they wanted me to know whatever it was, I would find out one day. I hoped it wasn't news that she was pregnant again. Hadn't they heard of birth control?

'I need your help, guy.'

'I'm broke right now, man.' As if I had ever asked him for money. I took a deep breath and let it out through my nostrils.

'That's a real shame. But *I'm* not broke. I need your help with something else. There is a picture of my cousin on your wife's phone. And my aunty has been saying she wants to put together a book with all the pictures of him since he was born. She has really been nagging me.'

'Then ask Bukky.'

'You know how your wife is – she will agree and then as soon as the kids need something, every other thought goes out of her head.'

'So you even know. I'm married to her, and I can't get her attention.' I rolled my eyes.

Since when did grown men begin to see their children as rivals? But this was the man she had chosen. I would never understand it. I mean, he supported Arsenal. It said something about the kind of man he was.

'I just need you to go through her phone and get a picture for me. That's it. Just help me – send it.'

He agreed, more to get me off his back than anything else. But I knew he would do it. Of the two of them – my sister and my brother-in-law – he was the more reliable.

An hour later, my phone vibrated. He had sent the pictures. It came through my sister's WhatsApp, but I knew he had been the one to search her phone and forward them. There were three photos. One was an ultrasound: the baby in the womb. The other two were of the baby as a newborn. His eyes were shut and he was attached to all sorts of machines.

I couldn't really tell if it was Remi. I had hoped that I would be able to see the yellow birthmark on his belly. But the picture was focused mostly on the baby's face, and it was also slightly blurry.

Besides, I had never been able to perform that trick people did, where they would look at a baby and tell you who the baby looked like.

Babies all looked the same to me. They had eyes that were always closed, no eyebrows, barely any hair. They never looked pleased to be here. They came in different colours, but that was about it. Besides, Remi was big now, he had more flesh.

There was a date on the ultrasound, but I wasn't sure if this helped me work things out either. Some babies came early, some came late; that much I knew. If I did the maths, then sure, the baby in the scan might be Remi. But it also might not.

Still, the picture might prove useful. If only to scare Esohe straight. Or Aunty Bidemi. I took a final swig from the whisky bottle.

Chapter Twenty

I jerked awake because I heard Remi crying. And there was something wrong with the cry. I went to Aunty Bidemi's room and hammered on the door. She opened it a minute later wearing a red silk robe. It was open and I could make out one of her heavily veined breasts. I wished she would cover up properly. The baby was asleep on her shoulder.

'Is he all right?'

'Why wouldn't he be?'

'He has been crying ...'

'What? No, he hasn't. He's asleep, look.'

'I heard him. I heard him cry.'

'Are you OK?' she asked.

'Yes! Are you sure he wasn't crying?'

'Does he look like he is crying to you?'

She showed him to me. He could not have looked more peaceful. And yet, I was still worried.

'In any case, I am meant to take care of him at night.'

'Fine. I'm tired anyway.' She placed him gently in my arms before shutting the door with a slam.

The slam woke Remi up and he began to protest once we entered my room. I walked up and down the room to get him to settle down but he resisted. I was still very tired. I couldn't remember when I had had a full night's sleep. He started to cry.

I sang all the nursery rhymes I knew to him till he calmed down, then I lifted his bum to my nose. Yes, there was something unpleasant going on there. Luckily, I now had a supply of nappies in my room.

He was patient with me while I stripped off his babygrow. He grinned at me as I opened his nappy and groaned. All the boy was drinking was milk. I was not expecting so much shit.

Most of him was a deep brown, browning more and more each day. But the blotch of yellow on his stomach stayed the same colour. It looked a little like the map of Africa. I told him it was because he came from kings.

When I returned to the bed with a new nappy, Remi greeted me with an arch of urine. It wet my lips.

'Thank you,' I told him. 'Pee was exactly what was missing from my diet.'

I cleaned us both up with wipes, and managed

to powder him and strap him up without getting peed on a second time.

Esohe had started shouting again. I could hear her rattling the door, screaming for us to let her out. We had left her in there for hours. She must have been worn out but she kept up the shouting.

Remi stared at me with large dark eyes, as though he needed me to tell him what was happening. I knew he could hear Esohe. Sometimes he would twist towards the sound. I flipped open my laptop and played songs from a kids' channel on YouTube, dancing about to try to distract him and myself.

Because I was drowning out Esohe's voice with the music, it took me a while to realize that my sister was calling my phone.

'Hello?' She was crying. I hadn't heard her cry in years. It made my stomach knot up. 'What's the matter?'

'Why did you tell him to go through my phone?'

'Tell who? Wait … Tunde? I didn't tell him to go through it. He was just meant to send me the picture.'

'Well, he went through it. And he found some pics.'

'What kind of pics?'

'You know what kind!'

'Why are you snapping at me?'

'Cuz none of this would have happened if you hadn't gotten involved.'

'How was I supposed to know you are cheating on your husband?' Even as I said it, I wondered how much I was to blame for my sister's actions. What kind of example had I been to her, and what would happen now? Men rarely forgave a cheating woman. I doubted I would be all that forgiving myself.

'I'm not cheating on him. I ... it was just pictures. Just me. I only sent one. I shouldn't have sent any, but I knew straight away it was a mistake.'

'You didn't delete the pictures?'

'Not everyone is a pro like you!'

I remembered that Bukky had no idea I had been tossed out by my girlfriend because of photos and messages that I had forgotten to delete. But I doubted telling her now would make her feel any better.

'What do I do, Bambi?'

'Calm down. How did he react?'

'He shouted and shouted. And he has locked me out of the bedroom. The kids are so upset and confused. And Bambi, I'm pregnant. I don't know what to do.' I didn't have a free hand to massage my forehead. I tried to sit on the bed, but Remi kicked off. He clearly wanted us to remain standing.

'Delete the evidence,' I told her.

'I just told you he has seen it.'

'And he will ask to see it again. Delete every naughty picture, every flirty message, anything from anybody that can be seen in a special way. When he calms down, you will have to play down what he saw. He won't be able to refer back to it, so he will begin to doubt himself.'

'Do you give a course in this stuff?'

'I'm trying to help you, Bukky.' She was quiet and then she started crying again. 'Promise him he can look at everything on your phone. In fact, if you think he'll believe it, claim that you took them for him. He didn't see the actual message, right?'

'No. Just the pics.'

'OK, so you can make him believe you took them for him, or just for some cheap thrills; but you were never going to send them to another man. Got it?'

'I don't know if I want to lie, Bambi.'

'You're a better person than me, Buks. You always have been. But I don't think this is the time for honesty.'

'You give terrible advice.'

'Will you be OK?'

She sniffed. 'I think so. Maybe.'

Chapter Twenty-one

On her second day, locked in the room, Esohe stopped screaming. In fact, there was no sound coming from her room at all. I knocked and called her name. No answer. She had to still be in there: there was no other way out. The windows had security bars on them – keeping thieves out and keeping Esohe in.

'She is just bluffing,' said Aunty Bidemi when I went to ask her for the key to Esohe's room. She was washing the clothes on the stoop in the garden. The washing machine had broken. There was a massive blue basin between her legs, and Remi's clothes were swimming inside them. She would pick one up, sprinkle washing powder on it, and give it a strong wash with her hands. She paused now and then to wipe the sweat off her brow.

I couldn't understand why she was choosing this moment to wash clothing outside. The sun was at its most intense. I had only been outside for five minutes, and I could already feel the patches of sweat in my armpits.

'I can't take that chance. Have you given her anything to eat?'

'No.'

'Aunty Bidemi, give me the key.'

'I'm thinking of the baby.'

'So you plan to keep Esohe prisoner till the lockdown is over?'

'You agreed that she was dangerous.'

'She needs food and water! Give me the key.'

She just shrugged and kept on washing.

I walked off and went to her room, planning to tear it apart if I had to, but when I got there I could see I'd never find the key. She had piles of folded traditional clothing in her cupboard. The key could have been slipped in between any of them. Or it could be in one of several carrier bags that she had stuffed with knick-knacks. And the key might not be in her room anyway. It would take me days to search the house properly. I was forced to return to her empty handed.

'What can I do to persuade you to give me the key?'

'You like her.'

'What?!'

'You men behave like fools when it comes to a small girl.'

'She is only three years younger than me, Aunty Bidemi. And I don't have any feelings for her.'

'Then leave her there.'

'Aunty Bidemi, see. I am opening that door. So you can give me the key and I'll open it like a civilized human being. Or you can keep it and force me to break that door down.'

She had aged. I noticed it in the many lines and creases as she scrunched up her face into the darkest look I had seen on her soft face. She dipped her hand into the gap between her breasts and dug out the key. I took it from her. It was warm.

Chapter Twenty-two

Esohe was sitting quietly on her bed when I entered the room.

Her room smelt strongly of her mint aroma and fly spray. There were clothes on the floor and on the chair and on her bed, hers and Remi's. There was a bowl of groundnut peelings on her dressing table as well as a couple of empty bottles of wine. I hadn't realized she was drinking so much. I noticed there were two half-filled baby bottles on the bed beside her. She didn't say anything to me. She just sat there, looking straight ahead. I suppose I was expecting her to run to the door.

'She won't lock you in again. I have the key now.'

She snorted.

'Are you OK?'

'How can I be OK?'

'I'm sorry, Esohe, but you forced us. You put sand in our food. You came into my room when

80

I was sleeping – I'm pretty sure it was you. You smeared the wall with blood ...'

'Blood? I admit that I did the sand in the rice thing. I was angry. But I didn't mess about with any blood. I swear!'

'Esohe ...'

'Why would I lie? Toh! You people have already locked me in here. You've stopped me seeing my baby. You have already judged me, found me guilty and sentenced me! What would I gain by lying now?'

It was a good point. She had nothing left to lose now by telling the truth. But if she didn't smear the blood on the wall ... Did she expect me to believe that Aunty Bidemi, who had knelt down and scrubbed at the blood with shaking hands, had put it there?

Our eyes met and she shook her head slowly.

'Please leave my room. I want to go and bath.'

'Esohe ...'

'Or do you want to follow me there? Do you want to watch me bath?'

I dropped the key on her dressing table and left the room.

Chapter Twenty-three

Mide called me again. It was beginning to feel like she was from another era. Only a week had gone by, but it might as well have been six months. I was finding it hard to recall her vanilla smell, the feel of her skin. I hadn't picked up the last three times she had tried me, but here she was calling again. She was keen.

'Hey.'

'Hey, what's up?'

'I … I'm just checking on you. I realized I don't even know where you are staying.' Was she worried that I might be shacking up with another woman? Why hadn't *I* thought of that?

'What does it matter where I am staying?'

'Look, you don't have to be an ass!'

'I'm just asking a simple question.'

'Sure.'

She didn't say anything, but she didn't end the call either. She was waiting for me to lighten the mood, but Esohe's words were weighing heavily on my brain. *What would I gain by lying now?* I thought of the baby who had died. And Aunty Bidemi feeding Remi with her large breasts.

'Are you still there?'

'What? Uh, yes. Yes, I'm here. Hey, Mide, listen. I have a question.'

'Yes?'

'If a woman doesn't breastfeed her baby, how long does the milk stay in her boobs?'

'What the hell kind of question is that?'

'Just answer me please.'

She paused.

'I guess like two weeks max.'

'Are you sure?'

'Yup. Pretty sure.'

'Can it, like, come back later?'

'Maybe … I don't know. Maybe you should Google it. I don't know anyone that's done that. What's going on with you, Bambi? Why are you asking about babies?'

'I'm just curious.'

She cut the phone, no doubt in a rage.

I checked the time – 3:50 p.m. It would be time for Remi to eat soon. He still drank milk from the bottle, but from the way he stared at me when I ate. It was probably time for them to start giving him solid food. Aunty Bidemi wasn't in her room and so I went to the living room. I could hear her singing.

Only it wasn't Aunty Bidemi who was singing. Esohe was cradling Remi in her arms. She did not look up when I walked in, she was too busy sniffing his skin. I knew she hadn't held him in days, and he did not seem to be in any danger, but I wanted so badly to take him from her.

Before I had a chance to speak, I spotted Aunty Bidemi to my right, leaning back on her sofa reading a Mills & Boon book. They were in the room together, and no one was pulling anyone's hair out. The scene, as peaceful as it was, made me nervous.

'Hey ...'

Esohe lifted her head briefly to smile at me, but Aunty Bidemi did not twitch. She turned a page of her book. Remi began to fuss and cry. Esohe resumed her singing.

'He is probably hungry,' said Aunty Bidemi from behind her book. 'Do you want to feed him, Esohe?'

'Yes, Aunty.' *Aunty?* When did she begin calling her Aunty?

Esohe took the bottle out of the warmer and sat down, while tilting the baby to ready him for feeding. I felt like a fool, just standing there, staring at them; but I was a little afraid to leave. Between these two lionesses, Remi was helpless.

I took a seat on one of the dusty armchairs, leant back and checked my emails and messages. Mide had sent me a very long rant about how she could do a lot better than me. I ignored her, and fired off a quick message to Bukky to check that she was all right.

'I need to change Remi's nappy,' said Esohe.

'The nappies are in my room,' replied Aunty Bidemi. I snapped my head up so quickly it caused me to crack my neck.

'OK. Thank you, Aunty Bidemi.'

Esohe left with Remi.

'What the hell is going on?' I hissed.

'What?'

'You're fine with Esohe now?'

'Oh. Yes. She has come to her senses.'

'What do you mean by that?'

'She has accepted that Remi is my child.'

'That doesn't make sense ...'

'Please, I'm trying to read.'

She returned to her chick lit, leaving me to think over our conversation. Esohe had come to her senses? I didn't believe a word of it. I stood up and went to find them. Esohe was blowing bubbles on Remi's stomach while he wriggled around on the changing mat. He smiled when he saw me, but the alarm bells in my head were still ringing.

'How is he doing?'

'He is good. He pooed a lot. Didn't you? Yes. Yes you did.'

'It must feel good to be able to carry him again.'

'It does. Aunty's being very kind to me.' She planted a kiss on his forehead, and then spun him over and powdered his butt.

'Esohe, what's going on?'

'What do you mean?'

'Only last night you told me the baby was yours. And now, you are saying Remi is hers?'

'I made a mistake. People are allowed to make mistakes.'

'Don't play me for a fool, Esohe.'

'I'm not playing.'

'I have a picture of Aunty Bidemi's baby. I can't be sure if it is Remi or not. But I'm willing to listen to all you have to say.'

She laughed. 'You're willing? Lucky me!'

'I want to know the truth, Esohe.'

She lifted Remi from the changing mat and raised an eyebrow.

'You are the only one who does not know the truth.'

Chapter Twenty-four

I rested my hand on the wall in my room. It was hot. The sun was baking the whole house. And there was no power again. It was like living in the Dark Ages. I sipped from a bottle of water and sat on my bed with my eyes closed.

Was this what it meant – to meditate? To allow yourself to be suspended in stolen time? And it was only a very little time. Whatever agreement they had come to would not last very long, I was sure of it. I took a breath—

Aunty Bidemi burst into my room. I let out the breath.

'Esohe told me that you have been asking her to say she is the mother of Remi.'

'That is not what I said.'

'She said you told her you have a photo that proves I'm not his mum!'

'Aunty Bidemi, I don't want to fight—'

'You are threatening me and my child and saying you don't want to fight?'

'I care about Remi as much as—'

'I thought Esohe was the problem in this house, but I did not realize the Judas would come from my own family.'

'Aunty, I don't know why he is trying to start trouble.' Esohe had been leaning on the door frame, looking at me smugly. She came and stood beside Aunty Bidemi, towering above her but so close that they looked like a two-headed monster. 'It is not even any of his business.'

'Wait,' I snapped. 'Of course it's my business. Remi is my—'

'Remi is what?'

'My cousin.'

'Is that what you wanted to say? Or have you started thinking you are his daddy?'

'Esohe, behave yourself!' I warned.

'So that is what this is all about?' she laughed. 'Have you been counting how many months have passed since we made sweet love?' I stood up, even though I had no idea what to do to shut her up, besides strangling her. 'Well, maybe you are the daddy. Maybe you're not. But you can't just claim a baby, you know. It's not 1000 BC!'

Aunty Bidemi looked from Esohe to me and back again. 'What are you talking about, Esohe?'

'Aunty, almost a year ago now, Bambi and I spent a very special night together. Didn't we, Bambi?' She even had the nerve to wink at me.

'Is this true, Bambi?' asked Aunty Bidemi.

'No. She is mad.'

'I can prove it,' slurred Esohe. 'He has a tattoo – of, like, a ship.'

This would not be the first time I would regret the day I had gone along with a dare, and let myself be tattooed. My friends had even rolled the dice on where and what the tattoo would be. But I could hardly complain, I had caused a number of their most awkward moments. In any case, I had never regretted it as much as I regretted it now. If you were a man that liked to have fun with different women, it was not a good idea to have any features that stood out. You didn't want anything that a woman could use as evidence, much as Esohe was doing now.

'Where is this tattoo?' asked Aunty Bidemi.

Esohe grinned. 'He'll have to take off his trousers.'

'Drop them,' my aunt barked.

'Excuse me?'

'I said, drop your trousers!'

'I'm not going to do that.'

'Why wouldn't you want to prove that you didn't sleep with your uncle's ... woman?'

'I shouldn't have to. And besides, even if I had a tattoo – and I'm not saying I do – she could easily have seen it by looking at my body while I was getting dressed. You saw yourself that she tried to force herself on me!'

'Liar, liar, pants on fire,' sang Esohe. 'Show us your big ship, Bambi. It's there, Aunty, on his thigh.'

'Drop your trousers!' my aunt shouted.

My thigh? I untied the strings of my sweatpants and dragged them down. I showed them my legs. The inside, the outside, the back, the front. No tattoos. No ships.

Esohe stopped singing. 'He's lying!' she shrieked. I didn't bother to comment. The evidence was doing all the talking for me.

'Hush!' Aunty Bidemi put her hand to her head and sighed. 'I'm sorry, Bambi. I'm sorry I doubted you.'

'We are all tense.'

'I don't know why I let her trick me like this.'

'I'm not lying, I—'

'Shut up! You just want me to think my nephew is bad like you. You cannot break up this family. Do you hear me?!' Having said her piece, she walked off, leaving Esohe and me to stare at each other.

'I don't know what juju you did, but I will find out.'

I didn't reply. I pointed to the door and watched her scuttle out like a spider. A poisonous spider. I closed it behind her and sat down on the edge of my bed. The afternoon sunlight was less fierce than before, the room a little cooler. I took a deep breath. I had the tattoo all right, but it was on my butt. Esohe had simply forgotten where on my body she had seen it.

Chapter Twenty-five

Esohe and I were close in age, so it was no real wonder that we went to the same places. And yet, I was surprised to see her at the club. Whenever I walked into a crowded room, my eyes would do a quick sweep. I would see where the bar was, which section was the VIP, check for anyone I knew, and spot the sexiest girls in the room.

Esohe was a head above most girls, so she was easy to spot. But the girl could also move. God hadn't blessed her with obvious hips, but she knew how to move what little He *had* given her. Her whole body was twisting. The dress she wore was silver and shone against her dark skin, and it was short, all the better to flaunt her long legs. I stood and watched from the bar as guy after guy tried to slip in behind her, to better enjoy the art of her moving hips, but she would simply twist away from them.

I only meant to check on her. She was my uncle's girl, and she wasn't even my type. I bought her a drink. She would have been a little thirsty after all that dancing. I had to squeeze myself through the masses of people. Half the drink had swirled out of the glass by the time I got to her.

'Bambi!' Her voice was breathless, husky. I handed her the drink. 'Thank you.'

'My pleasure.'

She drank and handed the glass back to me. I put it on a handy table. She had started dancing again. It was only natural that I join her. She didn't turn away from me. Instead, she began to twerk. I let her do her thing. It was just dancing. She wasn't even the type of girl I was attracted to. Her breasts were like apples, and a man didn't feel good unless he could hold on to watermelon-sized goods. But she wasn't wearing a bra, and it made me feel a little light-headed.

I hadn't come alone. I had arrived with a friend, but we both knew how it was. I glimpsed him now and again, and he would give me a thumbs-up. He didn't know who Esohe was. There had been no reason to ever mention her. After a while, I saw he had also found a girl to keep him busy. I returned his luck with a thumbs-up of my own.

I had not planned to spend my whole time with her. I figured I would dance with her once, maybe twice or three times, and then I would move on to another woman. But things don't always work out the way you plan them. We left the club together. I took her to a hotel close by.

Were there moments when I felt guilty? Yes. But the sum of those moments was not enough to hold me back. And besides, she wasn't Uncle Folu's wife. She was free to sleep with whomever she wanted to sleep with. My phone rang a couple of times – the woman I was dating at the time was clearly looking for me. But despite her generous body, she was not able to move as expertly as Esohe did, and so she was far from my mind.

That night was about Esohe and me.

Chapter Twenty-six

'Bambi!' Esohe screamed. 'Bambi!'

I sprinted from my bedroom and met her coming down the hallway. She was holding Remi in her arms and he was limp. Esohe kept on coming, holding the baby out to me. It was as though she were presenting an offering. I took a couple of steps backwards – I was terrified.

'I don't know what to do!' I cried.

'His skin is hot!'

So he was still alive, then. Yes, his chest was rising and falling. It was faint, but it was there, and as long as there was breath, there was hope. 'Give him to me,' I said, and she quickly slipped him into my arms. It was as though she was handing over her duty. He was so small. He was hot ... too hot.

'Run a bath, Esohe. Lukewarm water!'

She rushed off and I followed her, gently cradling Remi. 'It'll be OK,' I whispered, as much to myself as to him. When I got to the bathroom there were already several inches of water in the baby tub. I knelt down beside Esohe and dipped him into the water. He shivered but he didn't cry.

'What's happened?' I turned around to see Aunty Bidemi standing in the doorway.

'Help us!' cried Esohe.

Aunty Bidemi crumpled against the door frame.

'Is he going to die? He is going to die. I know it!' she cried.

'What?!' screamed Esohe.

'Can't you see? Neither of these babies are going to survive. My dear baby died! He died! And now Remi is being taken from us!' Aunty Bidemi was weeping and pulling her hair. 'Ah! He is going to die! I know it!' She was frantic.

I took the baby from Esohe and left the bathroom before Aunty Bidemi forced me to lose my shit. Esohe followed me and watched me as I tried to get Remi to drink a bottle of milk and then a bottle of water. We had baby Calpol, so I gave him some of that too.

She tried to speak to me while we waited for his fever to go down, but I wasn't replying. Fear wouldn't let me speak. Perhaps it was fear that was making Esohe talk so much.

'She is mad. I told you she is mad. She wants my baby to die,' she said.

And then,

'I named him Efosa because he is my wealth.'

And then she said,

'I gave birth to him here, you know. I wanted to go to the hospital, but because of the virus ... My doctor wasn't even picking up my calls. Aunty Bidemi helped me. She told me to push.'

I lifted Remi up. I was afraid to let him lie down for too long. He started throwing up. When he was more settled, I tried to call Uche but he wasn't picking up.

'What happened?' I asked Esohe.

'What do you mean?'

'Was he hot before you slept? Was he grumpy? Did he eat anything he shouldn't have?'

'Are you saying this is my fault?'

'No. No, I'm not. I am just trying to work out the cause.' I tried to keep my voice steady. I needed to find out what happened, more than I needed to lash out.

'He was fine. And then he was, like, crying and he felt really hot. He has been pooing a lot, too. Like a lot, a lot.'

'OK. OK.'

We watched over him. I tried to give him plenty of water. I searched Google endlessly, in order to find out what could be wrong with him. I looked for advice on babies with diarrhoea.

Eventually he fell asleep, but I went on searching. The internet offered me a solution. I went to the kitchen to make him a drink of six level teaspoons of sugar and half a level teaspoon of salt dissolved in one litre of water. I got him to drink a little when he was up, but he quickly fell asleep again.

I had never felt that kind of total, all-consuming tiredness. If I tried to nod off, fear would wake me and I would be alert once more. My eyes tired from watching his chest rise and fall. I prayed for the first time in ages.

Aunty Bidemi seemed to have moved on from her 'he will die' nonsense. She offered to watch him. But I did not bother to reply.

I was almost asleep when I heard him cry. Remi's cry was strong and beautiful. It broke my heart in a thousand different ways. Esohe was snoring. How could she sleep through such a wonderful sound? I managed to get him to drink some more of the sugar-water before he fell asleep again.

Uche finally called me back and I broke down Remi's condition to him.

'You're doing the right thing, Bambi. Give him the solution each time he poos. And remember to keep him watered. He will be fine in a couple of days.'

'OK. Good. But I don't even know why he was sick …'

'Just make sure you keep his bottles clean and you don't give him old milk.'

'We aren't newbies.'

He laughed at me and I couldn't help but smile.

'Stay safe.'

Chapter Twenty-seven

'Is he OK now?' asked Aunty Bidemi. I opened my eyes and knelt in front of the bed. He was fine. Esohe was also asleep, slumped half on, half off my bed.

'He is OK.'

'Do you need anything?'

'No.'

It wasn't true – we had run out of clean bottles. I walked about the house collecting empties. Most of them were in Esohe's room. It was as though she was allergic to the task of washing. Or any task at all.

There was a sour smell coming from one of the bottles. I brought it closer to my nose and took another whiff. And then another. The milk had gone bad. Had she fed Remi that milk? I couldn't find any bottle in her room that looked fresh. I looked around her room again, and saw that even Remi's clothes were unclean. When had she planned to wash them?

I put the bottle with the others and went

to the kitchen to sterilize them. Then I woke Esohe up gently and told her to go to her room.

'I'll take over from here.'

'You sure?'

'Yes.'

Chapter Twenty-eight

I packed my clothes into my suitcase slowly, afraid that I would be caught in the act. Even though I was fairly certain that both women were fast asleep.

I gave the room a once-over to see if there was anything I had missed. My charger was in my rucksack, along with my laptop and headphones. My wallet was still at Mide's. Getting my stuff together was the easy part.

I crept outside, opening the door as carefully as I could. Remi's freshly washed clothes were still hanging on the washing line. I grabbed all of them. Then I went to the store room to collect the unopened nappy bundles. I took his bottles and the sterilizer and put them in the boot of my car. The quiet made it so that every sound seemed three times louder than normal. I tried to get my hood to click without slamming it shut.

I went back to my room to find Aunty Bidemi standing there with Remi in her arms. What might I do to take him from her?

'What do you think you are doing?'

'I'm leaving with Remi.'

'And Esohe.'

'No. Just Remi.'

'You're not taking Esohe with you?'

'No. Why would I?'

Aunty Bidemi sighed. Her major concern seemed to have been about Esohe. She looked down at Remi and stroked his black curls. She brushed his forehead with a kiss.

'I really do love this baby. It is not as if I don't love him. I know you think I'm a bad woman. But I tried and tried for a child. And when I finally got one, he—' She began to cry. I should have felt sorry for her, but all I could think about was the safety of the baby in her arms. 'This girl opens her legs for *my* husband, and she becomes pregnant within months. Would you believe that he told me Esohe's baby would comfort me when my own baby...? He said this baby would bring us joy! He brought Esohe into our home. And then he died and left me with her!'

Her body was shaking. I worried that she would wake Remi up, and he would cry. Then his tears would wake Esohe up and we would be trapped in the house with them.

But Aunty Bidemi gave Remi another kiss and then handed him over to me.

'Bring him back to me when this is all over.'

'Yes.' I would have promised her anything. I left the house.

There was no car seat, so I was forced to use his baby basket and stuff it with blankets. I put the basket in the front seat, so I could use my hand as a seat belt when needed, and I drove really slowly.

I was taking a gamble. It was more than likely Mide would leave me standing outside her apartment block. So the sound of the door buzzing and unlocking was like a hymn in my ear. I pushed the door open and took myself and Remi into the lift.

When Mide opened her door, she looked at me and then at Remi.

'Bambi, for goodness' sake, you were only gone a week …'

Acknowledgements

Thank you:

To God, always, for the grace He has given me.

To Clare Alexander and everyone at Aitken Alexander – thank you for all you do for me and for my career.

To James Roxburgh, Kate Straker, Poppy Mostyn-Owen and everyone at Atlantic, for all the support, encouragement and hard work.

To Fanny Blake and Quick Reads, for the opportunity to be a part of this project.

To Temidayo Odunlami, for reading and listening and pushing me to do more.

To Folake Okuyemi, for taking the time to help me manoeuvre my way out of the medical corner that I had backed myself into.

To my family, for putting up with my eccentricities.

About Quick Reads

"Reading is such an important
building block for success"
- Jojo Moyes

Quick Reads are short books written by
best-selling authors. They are perfect for regular
readers and those who are still to discover the
pleasure of reading.

Did you enjoy this Quick Read?
Tell us what you thought by filling in
our short survey. Scan the QR code to
go directly to the survey or visit
https://bit.ly/QuickReads2021

Turn over to find your next Quick Read…

A special thank you to Jojo Moyes for her generous donation
and support of Quick Reads and to Here Design.

Quick Reads is part of The Reading Agency, a national charity
tackling life's big challenges through the proven power of reading.

www.readingagency.org.uk
@readingagency   #QuickReads

The Reading Agency Ltd. Registered number: 3904882 (England & Wales)
Registered charity number: 1085443 (England & Wales)
Registered Office: Free Word Centre, 60 Farringdon Road, London, EC1R 3GA
The Reading Agency is supported using public funding by Arts Council England.

Supported using public funding by
**ARTS COUNCIL
ENGLAND**

Find your next Quick Read:
the 2021 series

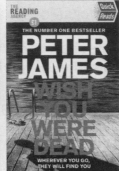

Available to buy in paperback or ebook and to borrow from your local library.

More from Quick Reads

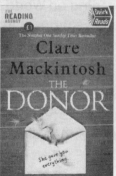

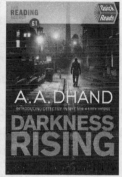

For a complete list of titles and more information on
the authors and their books visit

www.readingagency.org.uk/quickreads

Continue your reading journey

The Reading Agency is here to help keep you
and your family reading:

Challenge yourself to complete six reads
by taking part in Reading Ahead
at your local library, college or workplace
readingahead.org.uk

Join Reading Groups for Everyone to find a
reading group and discover new books
readinggroups.org.uk

Celebrate reading on World Book Night
every year on 23 April
worldbooknight.org

Read with your family as part of the
Summer Reading Challenge
at your local library
summerreadingchallenge.org.uk

For more information, please visit our website:
readingagency.org.uk

Read on for an extract of Oyinkan Braithwaite's
My Sister, the Serial Killer.

MY SISTER, THE SERIAL KILLER

WORDS

Ayoola summons me with these words—Korede, I killed him.

I had hoped I would never hear those words again.

BLEACH

I bet you didn't know that bleach masks the smell of blood. Most people use bleach indiscriminately, assuming it is a catchall product, never taking the time to read the list of ingredients on the back, never taking the time to return to the recently wiped surface to take a closer look. Bleach will disinfect, but it's not great for cleaning residue, so I use it only after I have first scrubbed the bathroom of all traces of life, and death.

It is clear that the room we are in has been remodeled recently. It has that never-been-used look, especially now that I've spent close to three hours cleaning up. The hardest part was getting to the blood that had seeped in between the shower and the caulking. It's an easy part to forget.

There's nothing placed on any of the surfaces; his shower gel, toothbrush and toothpaste are all stored in the cabinet above the sink. Then there's the shower mat—a black smiley face on a yellow rectangle in an otherwise white room.

Ayoola is perched on the toilet seat, her knees raised

and her arms wrapped around them. The blood on her dress has dried and there is no risk that it will drip on the white, now glossy floors. Her dreadlocks are piled atop her head, so they don't sweep the ground. She keeps looking up at me with her big brown eyes, afraid that I am angry, that I will soon get off my hands and knees to lecture her.

I am not angry. If I am anything, I am tired. The sweat from my brow drips onto the floor and I use the blue sponge to wipe it away.

I was about to eat when she called me. I had laid everything out on the tray in preparation—the fork was to the left of the plate, the knife to the right. I folded the napkin into the shape of a crown and placed it at the center of the plate. The movie was paused at the beginning credits and the oven timer had just rung, when my phone began to vibrate violently on my table.

By the time I get home, the food will be cold.

I stand up and rinse the gloves in the sink, but I don't remove them. Ayoola is looking at my reflection in the mirror.

"We need to move the body," I tell her.

"Are you angry at me?"

Perhaps a normal person would be angry, but what I feel now is a pressing need to dispose of the body. When I got here, we carried him to the boot of my car, so that I was free to scrub and mop without having to countenance his cold stare.

"Get your bag," I reply.

We return to the car and he is still in the boot, waiting for us.

The third mainland bridge gets little to no traffic at this time of night, and since there are no lamplights, it's almost pitch-black, but if you look beyond the bridge you can see the lights of the city. We take him to where we took the last one—over the bridge and into the water. At least he won't be lonely.

Some of the blood has seeped into the lining of the boot. Ayoola offers to clean it, out of guilt, but I take my homemade mixture of one spoon of ammonia to two cups of water from her and pour it over the stain. I don't know whether or not they have the tech for a thorough crime scene investigation in Lagos, but Ayoola could never clean up as efficiently as I can.

THE NOTEBOOK

"Who was he?"

"Femi."

I scribble the name down. We are in my bedroom. Ayoola is sitting cross-legged on my sofa, her head resting on the back of the cushion. While she took a bath, I set the dress she had been wearing on fire. Now she wears a rose-colored T-shirt and smells of baby powder.

"And his surname?"

She frowns, pressing her lips together, and then she shakes her head, as though trying to shake the name back into the forefront of her brain. It doesn't come. She shrugs. I should have taken his wallet.

I close the notebook. It is small, smaller than the palm of my hand. I watched a TEDx video once where the man said that carrying around a notebook and penning one happy moment each day had changed his life. That is why I bought the notebook. On the first page, I wrote, *I saw a white owl through my bedroom window.* The notebook has been mostly empty since.

"It's not my fault, you know." But I don't know. I don't know what she is referring to. Does she mean the inability to recall his surname? Or his death?

"Tell me what happened."